3 1994 00909 2302

MAR 1 8 1997

S... RY

D0605220

THE DOG WHO LOST HIS BOB

TOM AND LAURA McNEAL

ILLUSTRATIONS BY
JOHN SANDFORD

J PICT BK MCNEAL, T.
McNeal, Tom
The dog who lost his Bob
$15.95
CENTRAL 31994009092302

ALBERT WHITMAN & COMPANY · MORTON GROVE, ILLINOIS

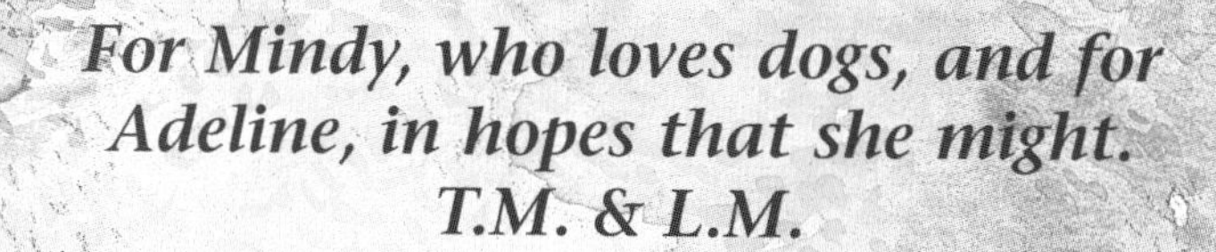

For Mindy, who loves dogs, and for Adeline, in hopes that she might.
T.M. & L.M.

For Bob Cusek, whose dog found him.
J.S.

The illustrator would like to thank Floyd and Bonnie Groen; John, Bill, and Eleanor Sandford; Kurt Mitchell; Lane Ann Bayless; Richard Cusek; Roisin Moran; and marvelous Marty Howard for their generous help in the making of this book.

The design is by Karen A. Yops.
The text typeface is Stone Serif.
The illustrations are rendered in watercolor and pencil.

Library of Congress Cataloging-in-Publication Data

McNeal, Tom.
The dog who lost his Bob / written by Tom and Laura McNeal; illustrated by John Sandford.
p. cm.
Summary: On Sunday when it is time for his bath, Phil runs away and spends months on his own wishing he could be back home, even if it means getting wet once a week.
ISBN 0-8075-1662-7
[1. Dogs--Fiction. 2. Lost and found possessions--Fiction.]
I. McNeal, Laura. II. Sandford, John, 1948- ill. III. Title.
PZ7.M4787937Do 1996 95-52932
[E]--dc20 CIP
AC

Text copyright © 1996 by Tom and Laura McNeal.
Illustrations copyright © 1996 by John Sandford.
Published in 1996 by Albert Whitman & Company,
6340 Oakton Street, Morton Grove, Illinois 60053.
Published simultaneously in Canada by
General Publishing, Limited, Toronto.

All rights reserved. No part of this book may be reproduced or transmitted in any form or by any means, electronic or mechanical, including photocopying, recording, or by any information storage and retrieval system, without permission in writing from the publisher.
Printed in the United States of America.
10 9 8 7 6 5 4 3 2 1

Willie and Phil lived at the farthest end of Bank Street, where the asphalt turned to dirt. Willie and Phil liked the dirt, but Bob, who cleaned windows all over town, did not. On Friday nights, Bob washed his green window-washing truck. Saturday afternoons, he washed the windows of his little gray house. And Sunday mornings, he washed Willie and Phil.

Willie didn't mind a bath, not even a hose bath on the driveway. Willie was a Labrador Retriever, which meant he could fetch ducks from icy lakes, if properly asked.

Phil, however, wasn't a Labrador Retriever. He was a bowlegged, warm-weather mutt who hated water. He hated lakes and dark clouds and garden hoses and, in general, all sources of wetness.

Every Sunday Phil tried something new to avoid his bath. Sometimes he pretended to be sick. Sometimes he hid under the bed. Once, when he pretended to be an ottoman, Bob just laughed and said, "What do you think, Willie? Isn't it about time we washed this furry old ottoman?"

One Sunday in August, when Bob was calling Phil for his bath, Phil did something he'd never thought of before.

He jumped through an open window. Willie barked and Bob yelled, "Phil!"— but Phil didn't stop.

He zigged and he zagged. He skeduddled and skedaddled. He slanted and he panted. He ran as fast and as far from Bank Street as a ragged, bowlegged dog could run, and he forgot to notice where he turned left and where he turned right. Soon he was in a place he'd never seen before.

When Phil stopped running, he could see it had turned into a summery, bath-free kind of day. He trotted down the sidewalk smelling this and smelling that. Before long, Phil found himself in an enormous park, where just about anyone would throw sticks for him to fetch. Boys in stiff baseball uniforms, joggers wearing headbands, and a tattooed man tossed sticks across the grass and watched Phil run. The only sticks Phil wouldn't fetch were the ones thrown into the sprinklers.

At dusk, when people started going home, Phil decided it had been the best day of his whole life. He ate a sandwich someone had left in the park, and a girl at Bongo Burgers fed him during her break. She learned that Phil would tilt his head sharply to the side if she said, "Would you care for one more potato fried Frenchly?"

After the girl said goodbye, Phil took his favorite stick and went back to the park. With nobody there, the park seemed big and empty and a bit scary. Phil kept his stick close by and curled up into his smallest self. He tried to go to sleep, but he couldn't. He wondered whether Bob and Willie were thinking about him. Finally he fell asleep watching the red taillights on the street below the park merge sleepily and fuzzily and sadly together.

In the morning, Phil started out for home. He missed Bob. But he didn't know how to get back to Bank Street. In all directions there were unfamiliar houses, unfamiliar trees, and unfamiliar parked cars.

All day long, Phil walked in different directions. He met dogs on leashes and dogs half-asleep on warm driveways, but none of them were Bank Street dogs.

Phil was hungry when he got back to the park, where two ribby dogs were knocking over trash cans. The dogs let out low, murmuring growls. One of them wanted to know what Phil was doing in *their* park.

Phil tried to explain that he was staying there for a while because he'd lost his Bob.

The ribbier of the ribby dogs told Phil that he was lucky he'd ever had a Bob to begin with. The other one began to tease Phil about his fancy leather collar, and then he snatched Phil's favorite stick. They scuffled, and Phil's collar pulled free. Phil knew he should wear it, but when he tried to put it back on, he couldn't. The ribby dogs skulked off, and to forget how hungry he was, Phil found a hollow under a hedge, lay down, and fell asleep.

In the morning, Phil decided the best thing to do was just wait until Bob found him.

But Bob's truck didn't come the next day or the next, and the way back to Bank Street remained as mysterious as ever. Phil crossed the street in front of a car that honked at him and skidded, just missing his back legs. He wandered into a yard that looked like Bob's, and an angry woman sprayed him with her garden hose. When he ducked away from the water, he strayed in front of a bus that had a horn even louder than the car's.

THIRD ST.
CHEESE

By autumn, Bongo Burgers had gone out of business and the nice girl had disappeared. Phil was always hungry. Wind blew the trees bare, snow fell, and Phil slept in a bed of wet leaves.

It occurred to Phil that at home he was wet only on Sundays. Now he was wet all the time, and the ice got between the pads of his feet and made them bleed. He decided if he ever got back to Bank Street, he'd take baths right and left.

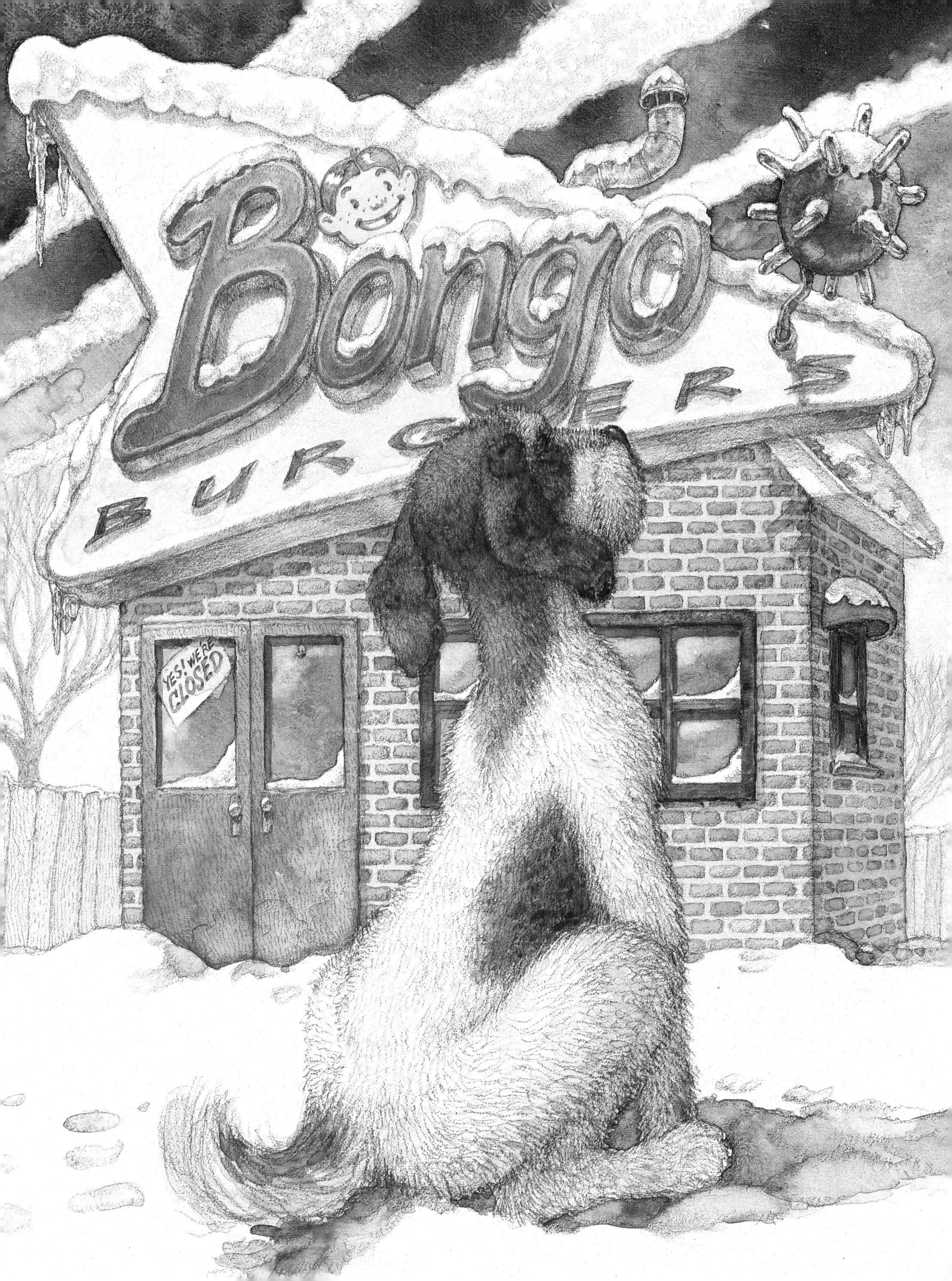
Bongo
YES! WE'RE CLOSED

Sometimes Phil would think he heard a truck like Bob's, but when he ran over, it would be someone else's truck. Phil would try to ask the humans if they knew his Bob, but they just thought he was a dirty, barking dog. In fact, the harder Phil tried, the more angry people got.

One time a boy opened a big can of blue paint, sloshed it on Phil, and said, "There. I guess you'll stop barking now."

One freezing afternoon, Phil saw a man in a muddy truck let the tailgate down with a thump. "Come on, Rosebud," the man said, and a German Shorthaired Pointer leaped out into the snow. When the man threw a Frisbee, the beautiful Pointer seemed to fly. Her coat was clean and smooth, and Phil knew it was soft. Phil's fur was rough and wiry and matted with blue paint.

"Come on," the man was saying. "Come on, Rosebud," and the Frisbee went sailing over the new layer of snow.

Phil touched the back of the man's leg, which smelled like cold denim and woodsmoke. "Hi, pal," the man said, scratching Phil's neck and ears. "Who are you?" Phil wanted to bark that he was Phil and he'd lost his Bob, but he just pushed his nose into the man's glove.

The man's shiny dog sniffed Phil, and he sniffed back. They chased the Frisbee and each other until Phil got too tired. "Here, 'Bud. Let's go, Rosebud," the man called.

When the Pointer jumped into the open truck bed with her Frisbee, Phil started to climb in, too. But the man eased him back down. "Sorry, pal," he said.

The man and the Pointer drove away. Phil ran behind the truck for a while and then just stood and watched.

He was curled up in the snow under a tree when he felt a nudge. It was Rosebud, and she led him back to the truck. He tried to jump in, but he missed, so the man lifted him in. Phil lay down in the back, and the truck began to move.

On telephone poles, the man posted flyers that said "FOUND DOG. Dec. 13th, Liberty Park Area." Weeks passed, heavy snow fell, and the wet signs bubbled and dried into a surface more like tree bark than paper. By the time Bob saw a flyer by the library, he could barely read the phone number.

Bob doubted that the found dog was Phil. Six months seemed a long time for Phil to survive on his own. Still, he called the number and left his name and a message on the answering machine.

FOUND DOG
Dec 13th
Liberty Park Area

Phil had tried to tell himself he had found a new Bob in Frank. But Frank's landlord wouldn't allow two dogs in the house, so Phil had to sleep in the garage. Rosebud would lick Phil's fur and try to get the blue paint off, but Phil always felt like a ragamuffin next to her. And he could never learn to catch Frisbees like she did. He preferred the taste of a stick.

So when Frank brought Phil into the house and played the message from Bob, Phil wagged his nubby tail like anything and tried to smell his Bob inside the machine. Phil got to hear Bob's voice three times: first while Frank and his girlfriend watched him sniff and wag, and two more times as Frank copied down the phone number. Phil started to leap and bark. Instead of scolding him, Frank and his girlfriend just laughed. Pretty soon Rosebud was barking happily, too.

CAYUGA
RIDGE

When Frank's truck turned down Bank Street, the smells in the air were familiar, and so was the gleaming square of Bob's front window, where Willie stood watching and wagging his tail. Then Willie began to bark. Frank did not quite have the tailgate down when Phil leaped out and ran up the steps to where Bob stood waiting.

Sunday is still bath day on Bank Street. But it is also the day when Bob takes Willie and Phil to meet Frank and Rosebud at Liberty Park, where the balls are for Willie, the Frisbees are for Rosebud, and the sticks are for Phil.